GRAVE
MESSAGE

GRAVE MESSAGE

MARY JENNIFER PAYNE

ORCA BOOK PUBLISHERS

Published in Canada and the United States
in 2022 by Orca Book Publishers.
orcabook.com

Library and Archives Canada Cataloguing in Publication
Title: Grave message / Mary Jennifer Payne.
Names: Payne, Mary Jennifer, author.
Description: Series statement: Orca anchor
Identifiers: Canadiana (print) 20210167106 |
Canadiana (ebook) 20210167149 | ISBN 9781459828643 (softcover) |
ISBN 9781459828650 (PDF) | ISBN 9781459828667 (EPUB)
Classification: LCC PS8631.A9543 G73 2022 | DDC jc813/.6—dc23

Library of Congress Control Number: 2021934068

Summary: In this high-interest accessible novel for
teen readers, Jaylin is surprised when she gets a text
message from a friend who died a year ago.

Orca Book Publishers is committed to reducing the consumption of
nonrenewable resources in the production of our books. We make every
effort to use materials that support a sustainable future.

Orca Book Publishers gratefully acknowledges the support
for its publishing programs provided by the following agencies:
the Government of Canada, the Canada Council for the Arts and
the Province of British Columbia through the BC Arts Council
and the Book Publishing Tax Credit.

Design by Ella Collier
Cover illustrations by Getty Images.ca/VectorFun
and Getty Images.ca/Big Ryan

Printed and bound in Canada.

25 24 23 22 • 1 2 3 4

MAR 18 2022

TL3/26/22

In memory of John Payne

and Roula Vasilopoulos-Schell

"A life that touches others goes on forever."

Chapter One

Jamal tries to hand the bottle of beer to me. "Come on, Jaylin," he says. "Just one drink."

I shake my head. "You know I don't drink. Besides, I can't stay. I have to study." I look down at my watch. "It's already eight thirty-five. I should've been home by now."

I look around the room. There are about twenty people from our school here. Even though we're in the middle of exams, the music is loud, and most people are up and dancing. The party is just getting started. No one seems too worried about studying. No one, that is, but me. Truth is, for most of the people here, exams won't be a huge problem. But what Jamal doesn't know is that for me, an English exam is like climbing Mount Everest. There's a reason I need a lot of time to study. And that reason is the only secret I've ever kept from Jamal.

Jamal rolls his eyes at me. "You're the smartest girl I know. You've been studying for this English exam forever. And it's not even for another two days. Don't you want to hang with me?" Jamal gives me the sad puppy-dog-eyes look.

"Honestly. I just…can't," I say. My mouth feels like I've eaten a big spoonful of peanut butter. I stand up and grab my bag. "I'm sorry. Call you later?"

Jamal shrugs. "Sure. If you can fit me in." He looks around the room. I know he's upset. We haven't spent much time together in the last few weeks. It's just a really hard time for me right now, and he doesn't get it.

I lean over and give him a fast kiss. "I'll call you," I say. I head across the room toward the front door. As I'm about to leave, I look back to wave goodbye to Jamal.

He's sitting beside Vicky Mars on the couch. Their heads are bent close together.

And they're laughing at something on her phone. Vicky puts her hand on Jamal's upper leg. My cheeks start to burn.

I've got to get out of here. Now.

I pull open the front door and race out to the sidewalk. Tears spilling down my cheeks, I run all the way home.

"Jaylin? Is that you?" Mom calls from the kitchen. "What have I told you about slamming that door?"

"Yeah. It's me," I say. I kick off my shoes and wipe at my eyes. I don't want Mom to see me upset. She already doesn't have much love for Jamal.

Mom wheels into the front hall. She looks up at me from her chair and smiles.

"Why are you standing out here? I've made your favorite. Pizza, with lots of extra cheese. Just the way you like it."

"I'm sorry, Mom," I say. I lean down and give her a kiss on the cheek. Her skin smells like warm vanilla. For some reason that makes me want to start to cry again. "I ate at the library with Alex. I'm super sorry."

Mom's brown eyes darken with worry. She knows I'm not telling the truth. I have not hung out with any of my friends for almost a year.

"Well, make sure you take a break at some point. I know this time of year is hard." She shoots me a sad smile as she turns her wheelchair around to go back to the kitchen. "And if you want to watch some Netflix with me tonight, I'd like that." She pauses. "I miss her too, you know."

"Maybe, if I get enough done," I say.

I go upstairs, lie down on my bed and open my computer. I still have to study. Our class has been reading *Dracula*—a novel I understand on a deep level. People think it's just about vampires. But the main theme is wanting the people you love to live forever. I get that. When you lose someone you really love, like I have, you'd do anything to keep them with you.

Time to hit the books. I've been given a version of *Dracula* that my computer can read out loud. Because I have dyslexia, when I'm reading my brain doesn't work the same as the brain of someone without dyslexia does. But it doesn't mean I'm not smart. I have the second-highest mark in my class. And I worked my butt off to get that grade.

After an hour of studying, it's time for a brain break. I check my Instagram first. There's a message. I need to see who has been sending me some Instagram love. It had better be Jamal. He's got some explaining to do.

I click on the message.

Hey, girl! I love you and I miss you. I know it must be a shock to read this. But it's me. For real. And I need your help. I need you to go to our spot tomorrow.

x Fatima

This must be a sick joke. Someone has hacked my best friend's account.

I slam my computer shut. My hands are shaking so hard, I have to sit on them just to think. Maybe I'm dreaming. Yeah, that must be it. I'll go to bed and everything will be okay when I wake up.

After all, there's no way this can be real. Because Fatima died exactly one year ago today.

Chapter Two

Bright sun hits my face. I bolt up in bed. What time is it?

I grab my iPhone off my bedside table. Nine o'clock? My exam starts in half an hour! How did I forget to set my alarm? Now I have zero time to review.

And that's when everything comes back

to me. The message from the sick person pretending to be Fatima. I whip open my computer. It's still there. My hands shaking, I slam my computer lid shut. I don't have time to deal with this right now. I'm late.

As I hurry to get dressed, I try not to think about last night. I need to focus on my exam. But it's super hard. First, Jamal letting Vicky be all over him at the party was bad enough. And then to have someone play such a sick joke on me? I don't want to block Fatima's account. It's one of my last links to her. But if I get another message like that one last night, I may have to.

I run downstairs. Mom's gone to work already, but I smile when I see she's stuck a note to the fridge, wishing me good luck. I grab a breakfast bar and a juice. Then I race out the door and hop onto my bike. I've got fifteen minutes to make it to school.

By the time I get to the exam room, I'm sweating like a pig. I have no time to fix my hair, so I pull my hoodie up. I wipe my hands on my jeans. Everyone is already sitting down. I get extra time to write tests and stuff, but right now that doesn't matter because I can't remember anything I've studied. I'm too stressed.

I scan the room. Could the person who sent the message be here right now? And if they are, how did they know about my and Fatima's secret meeting place?

"Phone, Miss Laws," Mr. Smith says from right behind me. I almost jump out of my skin. How did he sneak up on me like that? I spin around. He pushes up the glasses on his long, thin nose. Then he sticks an envelope and a cardboard box in front of me. "Phone," he says again.

"Yeah, yeah," I say, pulling it out of my back pocket. I turn it off. I don't want Mr. Smith creeping my photos. "How do I know it'll be safe?" I ask as I slip it into the envelope.

Mr. Smith rolls his eyes at me and sighs. "It will be safe, Miss Laws. Take a seat, please."

The only empty seats are in front of Jamal or beside Vicky. Great. I choose to sit near Jamal. That way he can find out fast that I'm ignoring him. Thing is, he's the only person I can talk to about the message.

"Seat, Miss Laws," Mr. Smith repeats.

I throw him some stink eye before I sit down at the desk in front of Jamal.

Right away I hear him move forward at his desk. "Jaylin? What's bugging you?"

The exam proctors are starting to move up and down the rows of desks, giving out the test papers. I take out my pen. I can't turn around or I'll risk getting kicked out of the exam. I'm allowed a memory aid, though, so I turn over the paper of prompts I made and write *Vicky Mars*! Then I hold it over my shoulder toward Jamal.

"Whatever," Jamal says. He sinks back into his chair.

As soon as I get my exam, I know it's going to be a disaster. I'm so stressed, I start to get what I call "the blur." Part of the reason for this is that my test is printed on the same paper as everyone else's. The bright-white paper is making it harder to read the words. They begin to jump and blur together.

At the two-hour mark, I stand up with everyone else. I only made it halfway through the test. But extra time isn't going to matter today. I can't think clearly enough to read. I'm just going to have to hope I get at least 50 percent on the exam to get my credit.

I grab my phone out of the box at the front of the exam room and head for the door. That's when Jamal grabs my arm. I pull away.

"What's your problem, Jaylin?" he asks. He looks tired. I wonder how late he got home last night and realize he didn't send me a goodnight text.

"Nothing," I say. I turn to go.

"I don't get why you're being so jealous," he says. "Vicky means nothing to me."

I stop walking and swing around to look Jamal in the eyes. "You want to know why I'm really upset? I'm upset because you didn't even stop to think that—on top of today's exam—it was also the anniversary of Fatima's death yesterday!"

Jamal's mouth drop opens. "Damn. I'm sorry, Jaylin."

"Yeah, well," I say. I turn on my heel and walk away. Fast. Fatima never forgot about the important things. Birthdays, special family holidays—she always remembered.

The warm sun hits my face as I step outside the front doors of the school. I'm not even down the steps when my phone beeps. Seriously? Jamal thinks I'm up to talking to him already? I tap the screen of my phone.

It's a photo of Fatima and me from our eighth-grade graduation. We're both laughing and stuffing cake into our mouths. I have blue icing all over my nose. Shaking, I sit down on one of the steps. My mom took this photo. I remember. There's also a message.

I know this is hard to believe, Jay-Jay. But it's me. Why didn't you go to our spot today? I need you to help me. You're the only one who can right what's wrong.

x Fatima

Jay-Jay. Fatima is the only person in the world who ever called me that. And she only did it when no one else was around. Is someone watching my every move? But I know I've got to go to our spot. Maybe whoever is sending me these messages will be there.

Chapter Three

Ghosts aren't real. This can't be happening.
But I can't get the texts out of my mind.
I hop on my bike and pedal as fast as I
can away from the school. Rather than
heading home, I take one of the bike paths
along the Don River. Birds sing at me from
the trees. The sun beats down on my skin.

Soon my T-shirt is sticking to my back. My eyes sting from the sweat that's rolling down my face. I take in every tree, every sound. I haven't biked this path since the last time Fatima and I came here.

I turn off the path. I'm now in a more wooded area. I have to get off my bike for this part and walk. The trees close in tightly around me. For a moment I think about going back. Why am I playing along with someone's sick joke?

Soon the forest opens up into a little clearing. It's almost a perfect circle of green grass and wildflowers. I look around. There's a tent in one corner of the open space. A few pieces of clothing are hanging on a rope strung between two of the trees. Someone is living here. I've got to be fast.

Our rock is still here. I don't know why I thought it might not be. It's large enough for two people to sit on. I walk over. This was our spot. Fatima and I spent hours and hours here. Sometimes we'd read or dance or watch videos on our phones. Our names, which we wrote on the side of the rock with a black felt-tip marker, have faded. But I can still see them. I count five steps toward the trees from there. It's where I need to dig.

My heart is beating like a drum in my chest. I've only got a metal spoon in my bag. I won't have to dig very deep, so it's okay. After a few minutes, my spoon hits something hard. I dig around the small metal box. Using my fingers, I pull it out of the ground.

I'm breathing so hard, I feel dizzy. Before opening the box, I look around. I'm not sure, but out of the corner of my eye, I think I see movement. It's only for a second, but I swear something moved by the tent.

Wiping the sweat out of my eyes, I fumble with the lid. The latch is rusty, but after a second it clicks open. Lifting the lid, I look inside. There it is. I reach in and pull out the small red velvet bag.

My hands shake as I open it. I turn it upside down over the palm of my right hand. Two silver necklaces slide out. For a moment the sun catches the metal, and they sparkle like stars in my hand.

I hold up the chains. A silver half of a heart sits on each. We loved the necklaces so much when we first saw them that we each bought two in case we lost one. These were the spares. Fatima wore one of the half hearts around her neck and I wore its match. I reach inside my t-shirt and touch mine. I've never taken it off since the day we bought them. I asked Fatima's family about hers after the accident, but her mom told me it wasn't with her clothes and things. Maybe it fell off in the ambulance.

Or maybe it was lost in the hospital when the doctors tried to save Fatima's life.

Tears blur my eyes. I wish I'd told Fatima I'd go to her place that night. She was so upset. Instead, I'd invited her over to mine to talk. That was the last time we spoke. She never made it to my house.

I take the necklace with the half heart that completes the one I'm wearing and put it on.

"Are you police?" a soft voice says behind me.

I jump up. The other necklace falls from my hand. It lands on the grass at my feet.

A man pops out from behind the rock. He's less than a foot away from me. How long has he been there?

"Are you the police? Are you looking for the girl that's been hanging around? Every day and night she's here," he says. He starts moving toward me.

"No. I'm not the police. And I don't know what girl you're talking about," I say. I begin walking backward toward my bike, not taking my eyes off him.

"The girl with the long black hair. Sometimes she dances with a red scarf that shines."

My blood runs cold. There's no way. This can't be happening. I begin to shake, even though the day is super hot.

"She's looking for her friend. She needs to give her a message," he says.

Ignoring the man, I grab my bike, jump on it and start pedaling furiously. I'm shaking so hard, I'm afraid I might fall off. My phone buzzes in my pocket. There's no way I'm slowing down to take it out. And I'm afraid to see who is texting me.

I bike home as fast as I can. The whole time, I pray my phone doesn't buzz again. Once inside I take a moment to catch my breath. I realize I'm starving. I grab a couple slices of pizza from the fridge and go to my bedroom. It's a good thing Mom isn't home. She'd kill me if she saw me taking food upstairs.

Between bites of pizza, I slide a wooden box out from under my bed. There's a red heart on top of it. I wrote Fatima's name over the heart, in gold glitter glue, on the day of her funeral. Before that day I'd never been to a funeral for anyone who wasn't really old. I open the box. Fatima's scarf is folded at the top. It was a birthday present. Her grandmother gave it to her for her tenth birthday. Fatima's older sister gave it to me. She said she knew Fatima would've wanted me to have it. I stare at it. The scarf is deep red with tiny silver sparkles. I shake my head. There's no way to explain what's been going on the last couple of days.

I take out my phone and check my messages. I'm hoping it was just Mom telling me she'll be staying late at work or something.

The first text is a picture of Fatima and me holding up our necklaces on the rock. We took that selfie the day we got them. Fatima's wide smile beams out at me. No one else has that photo. Neither of us posted it anywhere. This can't be real. I must be losing my mind.

I read the second message.

I need you to help me, Jay-Jay. You have to find out the truth about the night I died.

x Fatima

Chapter Four

Okay. I'm now Nancy Drew for a dead girl.

But not just any dead girl. For Fatima. My best friend. Forever.

I didn't sleep much last night at all. I tried to reply to Fatima. My text bounced back within seconds. I don't know why I thought it wouldn't. She's dead. Her phone number is no longer in service.

It's only five a.m., but I'm fully awake. I sit up in bed. It's still dark out. The early-morning sound of birds singing is starting. Other than that, it's silent. I look at Fatima's message again. What does she mean about the truth? There's no way she wants me telling her family the real reason she was coming to my place that night. So what am I missing?

I turn on the lamp beside my bed and grab my computer. It takes me only a couple of seconds to google the name of the man driving the car. Adam Green. The screen fills with links to different news sites and articles. I begin to read. There are photos of the accident scene— the fancy silver car and the red lights of the ambulance. Nearly every site also shows Fatima's school photo or a photo of her playing basketball. In one news story there's a picture of Adam Green helping little kids play baseball. He was the owner of a company that did something with computers.

Everything is there. All the facts. Green left a dinner party with his wife, Lisa, only a few minutes before the accident. His friends who hosted the dinner were very surprised. As far as they knew, he'd had only one glass of wine the whole night. But when the police came to the scene of the accident, they found a half-empty bottle of wine and some weed in the car. Green told the police he'd been trying to relax on the drive home. He said he and his wife had been fighting a lot. He pleaded guilty and ended up getting five years in jail. If he weren't white and rich, I'm pretty sure he'd be in jail a lot longer. But at least he's paying some price for taking Fatima from us.

I close my eyes. Fatima's wide smile comes back to me. What does she think people need to know about that night? And who would know anything more?

I open a Google doc and begin to type in the names of people who might have more information—Ann Potter, Adam Green, Lisa Green, the police. I'm sure the police aren't going to give me any secret information. And visiting Adam Green in prison, as a sixteen-year-old who isn't family, would be pretty hard to do. It would also mean driving two hours outside the city. And that would mean telling my secret to someone with a car.

But talking to Ann is easy. I can ask her to meet me today. It's Saturday, so I text her and ask if she can meet me at a Starbucks. Then I realize it's not even six a.m. Waking her up isn't a great way to start this. I hold my breath. After about a minute, my phone pings.

Sure. I can meet. What's up? Does 9 am work for you?

I text her back that everything's fine. It must seem odd to her to be getting a message from me. Ann and I were only friends, if you could even call it that, through Fatima. After Fatima's death, we talked for a bit and then Ann went back to her group of friends. Me? I stopped hanging out with everybody. For the first few months I stayed mainly in my room unless I was at school. Then I started to date Jamal. Hanging out with him had helped me push away the pain of Fatima's death…until this week.

"You're up early," Mom says as I walk into the kitchen. She's at her computer, with a giant cup of coffee. I know she's not reading newspapers. Mom is always working. She's a human rights lawyer, and she works harder than anyone I know.

"Yeah, well, I had some trouble sleeping," I say. I grab a mug and the coffee pot.

Mom looks up at me. She frowns. "You know how I feel about you drinking that," she says. "You're too young to get hooked on this stuff."

"Just this one cup today," I say. I add some sugar and milk to my mug. "I didn't sleep much at all. I couldn't get Fatima off my mind." That wasn't a lie. I've put my hair in a ponytail and thrown on a baseball cap. I know I look bad. I'm hoping that will make Mom feel sorry for me.

Mom sighs. "Okay. Try to take some time for you today. Maybe see a friend? Go for a bike ride?"

I take a long sip of coffee. "I'm going to hang out with Ann for a bit. Meeting her at Starbucks."

Mom raises an eyebrow at me. "Ann Potter? Really?"

I don't answer her. Instead, I look at the clock. "I better go. Don't want to be late."

As I'm riding to Starbucks, I try to think of what I'm going to say to Ann. I can't tell her the ghost of Fatima wants me to find out more about the night she died. So how do I explain why I'm asking her about that night after all this time?

Ann is already sitting outside when I arrive. Her red hair shines in the sun. She waves at me. It's more to let me know she sees me, rather than the kind of wave you give someone you're glad to see. That's fine. I'm doing this for Fatima.

"Hey, thanks for meeting me," I say as I sit down. She's already got me an iced coffee with whipped cream on top. I have to admit that was pretty nice of her.

"What's up?" Ann asks. She's playing with the straw in her drink. Maybe she's nervous too.

"What I need to ask you is going to seem strange," I say.

"Shoot," Ann says. She scoops whipped cream onto the end of her straw. Then she licks it off.

I take a deep breath. "I know that the night Fatima died, you two had a big fight. She was really upset. And that's why she was coming to my house. To talk about it."

Ann's head snaps up. She stares at me. Her green eyes are icy but also sad.

"What's the question, Jaylin? Because if you brought me here to make me feel bad, you didn't have to. I beat myself up about that fight every day." She stops talking. A tear slips down her cheek.

"No, that's not it at all," I say. "I just wanted to know if you knew anything else about what happened that night. Anything that wasn't in the news. I don't know...like something Fatima might've said."

Ann stares at me. "Why are you doing this?"

"I'm not trying to do anything," I say. I don't blame her for being mad. "She was just so sad that night."

Ann stands up. "You want to know what happened? Do you? I was on the phone with Fatima when she was hit by the car. I'd just told her to choose between her friendship with you and our relationship. And do you want to know why, Jaylin?" She's crying fully now. "I said that to her because I was jealous. I felt like she loved you more than me. I was worried she might've been in love with you… and not with me. And she got so upset… it was only a few seconds later that it happened. I heard everything. I could hear her crying for her mother. So, yeah, there's something you didn't know about that night. And ever since, I've blamed myself for Fatima's death."

Chapter Five

After Ann storms away, I sit for a moment in shock. This can't be what Fatima wanted me to find out. I feel a bit sad for Ann, but mostly I feel angry. I can't believe she asked Fatima to choose between her and me.

I knew why Fatima was coming to my house to talk about the fight that night. Ann was her first girlfriend. Fatima was super nervous about telling her family she was gay. I was going to be with her when she did it. She really liked Ann a lot. And even though I knew Ann didn't really like it when I was around, I wanted Fatima to be happy. Fatima had planned to tell her family about Ann that weekend. Now I knew why the fight had her so upset.

I glare at the iced coffee. I want to throw it against the wall, but I'm too thirsty. My phone pings, and my heart jumps.

Jay-Jay, go to 98 Lookout Drive. There you will find what you need.

x Fatima

I stare at the text. What if all of this is a dream? What if I've lost my mind? Maybe I should just go to a hospital.

My phone pings again. There's a photo of Fatima and me when we were about ten years old. She's holding her puppy, Roger. It was the day she got him from the shelter.

Tears fill my eyes. I laugh. "You really know how to make me feel bad, don't you?" I say out loud. Two women sitting at the table next to me look over. I smile back at them and wave. They quickly look away. I'm just a girl talking to her dead best friend, I want to say. Nothing to see here.

Sitting back in my chair, I take a long sip of the coffee. Then I google 98 Lookout Drive. A photo of a giant house comes up. It's in a very rich area of the city. It's also at least an hour's bike ride away. Super strange. I'm pretty sure Fatima was never in that neighborhood. I sigh. It's crazy hot out. Still, I can't let Fatima down—or the ghost of Fatima.

I text Mom and tell her I'm going to the beach with Ann for a few hours. Then I turn my phone off because I know Mom's going to text me. She would find it hard to believe that I'd be with Ann all day. She'll call me out on this lie in a second. Sometimes it's tough having a mom who cares so much. I hop on my bike and head west toward a much quieter part of the city.

It takes me forty-five minutes to get to Lookout Drive. The houses are as big as hotels around here. Green parks and fancy cars are everywhere. I pull my bike up onto the sidewalk and sit down on a bench. I really need water and wish I'd brought some with me. Pulling out my phone, I use the reverse address lookup to find out who lives at number 98.

Lisa Green.

My heart stops. What does Fatima think I will find here? I mean, I can't just walk up, ring the doorbell and ask to search their house. And I spoke at Fatima's funeral and was quoted in at least one newspaper. That means there's a good chance Lisa Green knows who I am.

Still, I've come this far. I have to trust Fatima. There's a bike rack near the bench. I lock my bike there and take a deep breath. Then I walk toward the house. There's a tall gate at the end of the long drive. I stand for a moment on the sidewalk and look around. It's not too late to turn around and leave. I'm starting to feel like I need to pee.

I take my phone out of the pocket of my backpack and turn it on. Right away it pings. I jump. Can Fatima be watching me in real time? I look at the screen. It's Jamal.

Jaylin, I'm sorry I wasn't there for you about Fatima. Can u talk? Meet at basketball courts at 4?

It's already nearly noon. I text him back that I'll be there, even though I have no idea what's going to happen in the next few minutes with Lisa Green. I mean, I don't even know if she's home.

There's a doorbell on the gate and what looks like a camera above it. I pull my baseball cap down lower. That way my face isn't as easy to see. Then I press the bell.

After about a minute there's a clicking sound. "Hello?" a woman's voice says.

"Amazon," I reply. I try to lower my voice to sound older. Biting my bottom lip, I wait for her to answer.

"Drop it at the back door," she says. Her voice sounds strange. I can hear a little kid crying. There's a buzzing sound, and the gate begins to swing open. I walk in.

Chapter Six

It takes me about five minutes to walk up the long driveway to the back of the house. That's how big it is. The grass and trees around the house are perfect. I stop for a second and look around. I wish Mom had a backyard like this to relax in.

After I ring the doorbell, I stand to the

side of the door. That way Lisa can't see me when she first looks out.

"Who's there?" a voice calls out from the other side of the door. She doesn't sound happy. I can still hear the crying child. I don't answer though. I need her to open the door.

"I said, who's there? What the hell?" I hear the door opening. Lisa peeks out. She looks pretty rough. Her bleached blond hair is messy. She has on yoga pants and a white T-shirt that's stained. You'd think with all her money, she would look a lot better. Or at least clean.

I step in front of her. "Lisa?" I ask.

She looks at me. "Who are you? Do I know you?" she asks. Her words come out funny. Then the smell of her breath hits me like a slap. I know that smell. She's been drinking. A lot. I glance at my phone. It's only twelve fifteen.

A tiny face peeks out from beside Lisa's leg. The child's cheeks are wet with tears. Snot runs from her nose to her lip. "Mommy? Hungry," she says.

"I said you need to wait," Lisa says to the child. Her voice is cold.

I smile at the little girl and wave to try to make her feel better.

"Like I said, do I know you?" Lisa asks again. This time she folds her arms across her chest. She glares at me.

"I'm not sure," I say. "But I was Fatima Lopez's best friend."

Lisa's eyes grow big. "You need to leave," she says. She starts to close the door.

I stick my foot out to stop her. I'm glad I wore my combat boots today.

She glares at me. "Do you want me to call the cops? Really? Likely won't turn out well for you."

Her words hit me like a slap. I need to think fast. I reach into my pocket and start to record.

"I know there's something that's been kept secret about Fatima's death. About that night," I say.

Lisa stops. She stares at me. "What do you mean? Who told you?"

"I can't tell you. I promised not to," I say.

This is not the time to start talking about ghosts.

"Did he tell you? What did you do, write him? I knew Adam would betray me." She's shouting now and talking more to herself than to me. It's a good thing the houses are all so far apart here. She's really loud.

I have to play along to get her to talk. "Yeah, he told me," I say. "You want to see the email? If I can still find it..." I'm hoping she'll just tell me what she thinks I know.

She looks at me. The anger leaves her face. "Sure," she says. "Why don't you come in? You must be thirsty. It's so hot out."

"No, that's okay," I say. There's no way I want to be around this lady longer than

I have to be. Though I do need to pee. And badly.

"Just for a minute. Please. I was rude before, but I would like to talk about this," Lisa says. "I also need to give Rose her lunch."

"I do need to use the bathroom," I say.

She opens the door wider. "Of course. Come in. Our cleaning lady hasn't been here today, so excuse the mess."

I pause for a second. She's being so friendly now, it's throwing me off. But I need to find out what she thinks her husband told me about the night of the accident. And I need the bathroom.

I walk inside and follow Lisa and her daughter up a set of stairs. Everything is fancy. There's artwork everywhere. It's like being in a museum. It's also pretty messy for a rich person's house. I spot a few bottles of wine. Some are empty. Others have some wine left in them.

"It's just down the hall. At the end," Lisa says as we enter a huge kitchen. There's an open bottle of wine and a glass on the table. She points to my right.

I get to the bathroom and quickly close the door. I'm not sure how to get Lisa to tell me the secret she and Adam are hiding.

As I'm washing my hands, there's a loud click at the door. I jump. I try to open it, but I can't. I bang on the door a few times.

"Sorry, Lisa? Lisa? I think the door is stuck," I yell.

"It's not stuck, Jaylin," Lisa says. She's right on the other side of the door. "It's locked. I locked you in. Guess what else? They don't allow emails in prisons. That's where you messed up. I knew Adam didn't send you an email. He couldn't have. And you couldn't have sent one to him."

I press my face up to the door. "Let me out," I say. "Please. I'll leave you alone. I promise."

"I need to know who told you about that night," she says. "Because only Adam and I knew. That means he told someone else. And then they told you."

"I was lying," I say. I'm trying not to cry, but I'm really scared. "I don't know anything. I swear."

"Well, I don't believe you. I think you know that I grabbed the wheel that night when Adam was driving. We were fighting. But I didn't mean to kill your friend. She stepped right out in front of us. It was so dark out. And she was on her phone. It was her fault."

I let out a long scream. This woman is evil. I can't believe she's saying such horrible things about Fatima.

"Now, now, Jaylin. I guess you know that Adam took the blame for me. Told the police that my wine bottle and the drugs in the car were his. He did it because I was pregnant with Rose. He didn't want our baby born in prison. That's what you do when you love someone. Isn't it?

Adam would die for me. You loved Fatima, right? You came here thinking you could trick me. That shows you're willing to die for her."

Her words hang in the air. Now I'm super scared. "Please let me out," I say. I'm begging now. "I promise I'll never tell anyone about this." Tears roll down my cheeks.

"I guess you should've thought about that," Lisa says. "I'm going to tell the police you broke into my home, if you call them. I'll say that you threatened me and my child." She goes quiet. "I'm going to go and make lunch for Rose. But I'll be back soon."

I slide down the door and cry into my hands. If I call the police, I don't know what she'll say or maybe even do to me. My phone pings. It's Mom.

What time did you say you were going to be back? Want to have a movie night? Love you.

I start to cry harder. Why did I come here? What was I thinking? Ghosts aren't real.

My phone pings again. I better put this thing on silent. I'm afraid Mom might try to call. I look at the screen.

You've been recording Lisa this whole time. Let her go to the kitchen. There's a window above the toilet. Use it to escape. There's not much time. Go!

x Fatima

Chapter Seven

I wait about a minute to make sure Lisa isn't still outside the door. Then I get up and hurry to the toilet. There's a long, narrow window above it. I climb up onto the toilet tank, hoping I'm not making too much noise.

Once I'm at eye level with the window, I realize just how narrow it is. This is going to be tight. I slide it open and look out. The bathroom is on the second story of the house. Fatima was smart to tell me to go to this window. It looks out over the front lawn of the house. I can see the street from here. It's a pretty big jump though. And I'll also have to run to the gate. Hopefully it opens from the inside. And hopefully Lisa won't see me.

Pulling myself up, I start to wiggle through the window. I'm going feet first so that I don't land on my head, but it means I can't see behind me. I get to my hips and bum, and things get tight. I stop for a moment. What if I get stuck? That would help make Lisa's lie about me breaking into her house look true for sure.

I take a deep breath and push hard with my hands. There's a burning pain as my flesh is squeezed through the window frame. Then I'm falling, trying to figure out how to land so I don't break my neck. I crash into a row of bushes. Twigs snap and scratch at my arms and face. I lie there for a few seconds, trying not to breathe. Did Lisa hear me fall?

Then I jump up and begin to run as fast as I can. The gate seems so far away. As I get closer, I begin to pray it will open from the inside. If it's locked, I'm done.

I reach the gate and push it. It swings open. I run down the sidewalk, back to the park where I left my bike. I know I don't have much time. Lisa will come after me. I know too much.

Hopping on my bike, I pedal madly away from Lookout Drive, going as fast as I can. But I'm not heading home. If Lisa Green follows me, or if she somehow has a way to find out where I live, that will put Mom in danger. I'm not going to chance that.

Instead, I head to the basketball courts. After I've been riding for a while, I stop and text Jamal. And then I text Mom. Before biking back onto the street, I look around to make sure no one has been following me.

I don't relax until I pedal around the corner of the school into the parking lot and see Mom's van. Then, as the basketball courts come into view, I see Mom, Jamal and a police cruiser, and I get nervous again. An officer is speaking to both of them. I pull up on my bike. Both Jamal's and Mom's eyes grow big.

"What happened to you?" Mom cries. She reaches up and gently takes my hand. My arms are covered with scratches. Some are so deep, blood is still dripping from them. "It's fine," she says, seeing me looking at the police officer. "I called Officer Edwards. He's here to help us."

I pull out my phone. "I'm okay. I fell into some bushes. But I need all of you to listen to this." Then I press Play on my phone and let Lisa Green tell her secret to the world.

Chapter Eight

It's been two weeks since everything happened. The media camped outside our house for days after the story broke. It was hard for me to explain why I went to see Lisa Green. I told everyone that I'd had a dream about the night of the accident. I said it was like Fatima came to me in my sleep. It's not a total lie.

I bike to our spot. The tent is still here. This time the man is outside. He's built a small fire and is cooking something over it. He looks up as I get off my bike. I'm not scared though.

"You're back," he says. "Are you hungry? I've got enough beans and hot dogs to share."

"I'm good, thanks," I say. "Sorry to bother you. I'm just here for a few minutes. It will be the last time. I just wanted to sit on this rock for a bit. Is that okay?"

He smiles. "Of course. This land is for all of us," he says. "I put the necklace you dropped back into the box. And the box back in the ground." He pauses. "It's good you came back. Your friend has been waiting to see you. I'll eat my dinner in my tent to give you some space."

I go to the rock and sit down. The sun is bright. I lie back and close my eyes. A warm breeze washes over me.

"Thank you, Jay-Jay," Fatima says.

I sit up. She's here. Fatima is sitting beside me on the rock. She's wearing her red and silver scarf. The one I have at home. And her necklace. The sun shines through her and all around her. She smiles.

"Thank you for making things right." She reaches out and touches my cheek. It feels like a cool wind. "Take care of my family. And Roger. Tell Ann she is not to blame."

I nod. "I will. I promise. I miss you so much," I say. Tears roll down my cheeks.

"I wish I hadn't invited you over that night. Please don't go. Don't leave me."

Fatima smiles at me. "Move on and make new friends, Jay-Jay. You are the best friend anyone could ever have." She looks around. "I will always be here. In every sunrise, in every bird's song, in the sound of ocean waves..."

I open my eyes and sit up. There's a little red bird on the rock. It's only inches from my leg. It looks at me and chirps. Then it flies to a tree.

I smile and pull out my phone to text Mom.

Want to have a movie night? I'll make the pizza. Can I invite Alex? x

Acknowledgments

I want to thank everyone at Orca Book Publishers for helping to bring this book and many other hi-lo stories to life. Thank you to my editor, Tanya Trafford, for her insight with the story. I am grateful for the continued support of my agent, Amy Tompkins of Transatlantic. As always, thank you to my partner, Robert Stewart, for his constant encouragement and companionship—especially during the pandemic.

DON'T MISS THESE OTHER THRILLING READS!

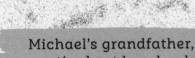

Michael's grandfather, a retired cat burglar, helps him steal back a valuable necklace.

Something is oozing all over the city. What is going on and how can Bran stop it?

Matt makes a startling discovery that he hides from his abusive foster parents.

Mary Jennifer Payne is a graduate of the Humber School of Creative Writing and the author of a number of works for young people, including the Orca Soundings title *Enough*. She works as a special education teacher and lives in Toronto.

For more information on all the books

in the Orca Anchor line, please visit

orcabook.com